About the Author

My love for language and storytelling was born at a very early age when I realized my love for language itself. This led me to pursue an academic career in language-related fields. After two university degrees I can safely say that my love for language still goes strong and has not dimmed even in the slightest. This book is meant to be a first step into a much larger career path and also a contribution to those who enjoy short stories.

This is a work of fiction. Names, characters, businesses, places, events and incidents are either the products of the author's imagination or used in a fictitious manner. Any resemblance to actual persons, living or dead, or actual events is purely coincidental.

QUATTUOR IV:
THE BOOK OF AURELIUS

CHRIS KAYEL

QUATTUOR IV: THE BOOK OF AURELIUS

Vanguard Press

VANGUARD PAPERBACK

© Copyright 2023
Chris Kayel

The right of Chris Kayel to be identified as author of
this work has been asserted by him in accordance with the
Copyright, Designs and Patents Act 1988.

All Rights Reserved

No reproduction, copy or transmission of this publication
may be made without written permission.
No paragraph of this publication may be reproduced,
copied or transmitted save with the written permission of the
publisher, or in accordance with the provisions
of the Copyright Act 1956 (as amended).

Any person who commits any unauthorised act in relation to
this publication may be liable to criminal
prosecution and civil claims for damages.

A CIP catalogue record for this title is
available from the British Library.

ISBN 978-1-80016-819-0

*Vanguard Press is an imprint of
Pegasus Elliot Mackenzie Publishers Ltd.*
www.pegasuspublishers.com

First Published in 2023

**Vanguard Press
Sheraton House Castle Park
Cambridge England**

Printed & Bound in Great Britain

Dedication

This story is dedicated to my parents and close friends without whom this wonderful work would never have existed.

Acknowledgements

A big thank you to those closest to me who allowed me the time to create something I have always wanted but never had the time for and for also sticking by me and encouraging me to fulfill my dreams throughout my life.

THE WAY HOME

It must have been around eight-thirty p.m. and I was positively anxious and looking forward for the date to come. As you might expect I had spent almost two hours getting ready for the date with the woman of my dreams at my most favorite place in this world. It wasn't just that I had finally managed to book a date after months of continuous work; I was also going to announce my greatest victory yet. I'm sure she would react to the news in the appropriate manner and my excitement as she had done so many times again in the past. Our passion for success and a loving relationship were only two of numerous factors that would constantly pull us together despite our differences and wants. She was the one for me despite all the walls that were erected between us; we were star-crossed, in a way. Two different classes, two completely different individuals filled with such hopes and dreams that could potentially take the world by storm.

Early in the morning of the same day I had woken up with a heavy sense of impending doom pulling me in every direction, but as always, I shrugged it off and decided to make the absolute best out of the day ahead. *All is fine. All will be ok. Don't worry about a thing.* To this day I still don't recall how many times I made the same utterances in my head, but never actually vocalized them. I imagine even the bathroom mirror would slap me if it had arms just out of pure rage for seeing me repeat the same thoughts in my head while getting ready for work. *Was I ready for what was to come that day? Did I know of what would follow the initial events of that day?* I can surely tell you in retrospect that I would not. The only undeniable fact was that I got to wake up in such a beautiful house every day and enjoy the freedom my financial status would afford me. My family was away and by *away,* I mean light years away, though not a single day would pass without me wanting to reach out to them, but the daily grind and our pact would prevent me from acting upon any such desires. After my morning run and usual grocery shopping, I returned home only to find Robert waiting for me by my front porch door begging to be let in. Robert was a stray Devon rex I happened upon about a year ago. My love for all creatures and the need to take care of another creature other than myself were the two things that made me allow him to stay and indulge his adorable stubbornness and constant neediness.

I opened the door and he dashed under my legs to his feeder.

"We both know who the owner is in this house, don't we, buddy?" I muttered to myself. As I was arranging the groceries in the refrigerator, I could hear Robert purring with excitement and satisfaction. It took

me about thirty minutes to arrange everything. By the time I was done, Robert had finished and had already run to the door ready to demand to be let out the moment I crossed the foyer leading to the main door. Knowing what was coming, I opened the door and expected him to run out like a bullet, which he did until it was time for him to see me the same night to repeat our usual routine. Immediately after that, I rushed to the living room to grab my phone and start my daily phone calls knowing full well I had to get in my requisite ten hours of phones calls in order to make sure everything was running smoothly with my supervision, of course. The first call was to the bank, then the company lawyers were the inevitable second, accountants and assistants were to be the ones coming organically after the first two. Calls in the life of one as busy as me were the holy grail of organizational tactics. The day before and each day before the next the phone calls and errands would have to be mapped out to perfection to fit my insanely busy schedule. Even the slightest deviation from my schedule could throw off the entire month and mess up everything.

It goes without saying that in order to get everything done on time the day would have to mandatorily begin at six a.m. the latest, otherwise other people from the company would have to take the reins shortly in order to settle everything and, quite honestly, I have always been reluctant to allow such a thing. I often told myself that it wasn't a matter of trust, but rather my unique way of having a perfect overview of all my business arrangements. I will never forget the state of my house that day; it was as if something that had just jumped out of a horror story. Though the house was more reminiscent of a clinic rather than a house due to how the housekeeper adhered to her schedule and never deviated from it, not once, the living room was covered in legal paperwork, bills, and financial statements from ground to ceiling. You simply couldn't walk from one room to the next on the ground floor without tripping some paper pile. That was just the start to my day given how everyone at the company was depending on my closing the deal to acquiring a new company that would add to our portfolio and diversify our public presence in the market. Now that I come to think of it, I was more stressed than anyone else, simply because I felt the pressure of keeping my company viable all the while making sure that my employees would not lose their job due to budget cuts. I wouldn't feel comfortable knowing that I would be forced to let people off simply because it wouldn't be viable for the company to keep them on the payroll. At twelve o'clock sharp, the much-awaited call came. It was Jonathan Matthews, founder and CEO of the company I was meant to acquire for a year and a half, and, who after a long negotiation period, had agreed to sell and step down as CEO. I let the phone ring three times before I picked up. Those ten seconds were torture, but at the same time an inexplicable wave of optimism washed over me, and it was in that moment that I was going to succeed and finalize the deal.

"Good afternoon, Mr Aurumstein," he said in a calm voice.

"Good afternoon, Mr Matthews," I replied in a similarly polite manner.

"I had my lawyers draft the final contracts this morning. I could send them over to you in a few minutes," he continued.

"That would be amazing. It has been an honor doing business with you," I added.

"Same goes for me. I'm sure your vision for the company is exactly what the public wants and deserves at this point," he closed.

"I couldn't agree more," I replied confidently. "Thank you so much for notifying me on such short notice. I will have my lawyers check the draft, sign it electronically and send over the finalized paperwork," I added and followed with *have a wonderful day.*

The goal had been achieved. In just under a few hours I would be 4,000,000 dollars richer thanks to the liquidation of the company's stocks. I was over the moon and for a brief moment I had forgotten the knot in my stomach and the excitement of success had taken over completely, but the feeling of dread was still there looming over my head like the axe of the executioner ready to fall and sever the head of the accused. My excitement and ever-charging desire to never stop and continue working and building my future pushed aside the feeling of dread yet again and forcefully gave way to the rest of the day.

I rushed upstairs to shower and call Stefania, my date for that night and the woman I was sure I would spend the rest of my life with. The phone just rang once, and she picked up filled with glee before I ever announced the good news.

"Did you do it, babe?" she said. "I know you did it. You couldn't have miscalculated even if you tried," she added without a hint of doubt in her voice.

For a split second I was taken aback by her unwavering faith in my abilities and resolve. Despite knowing her for almost three decades, I was always in awe of how someone as amazing and trustworthy as her was in my life. I paused for a few seconds for dramatic effect, and then exploded.

"I freaking did it," I said with such joy even I couldn't believe.

"I knew you could do it. You have been working so hard on this for a year and a half. You deserve the success and hopefully now some respite even though I know how you hate to leave work behind," she continued with a slight hint of sadness.

"Don't worry. Tonight is our night. Nothing will change our plans and from now on I promise I'll take more time off work and spend it with you," I said.

"Great! I'm so glad to hear that. See you tonight then and wear something dashing. I have a surprise for you after dinner. See you at our favorite restaurant at nine p.m."

"See you tonight, beautiful!" Looking forward to it," I replied with a slight tinge of horror that had not still left me despite the excellent turn things had taken that morning.

After about ten minutes of a relaxing shower, I decided to go downstairs get something from the refrigerator and sit on the front porch and relax a little before jumping back into work. As I took the last step of the staircase, I walked through the main living room to get to the kitchen of the ground floor. I paused as I walked past the fireplace where above the mantle towered a gigantic painting of my father and mother. That painting had been there since I could remember. *It was their way of looking out for me* I told myself many times. This painting truly held such a huge place in my heart, but I could never tell anyone who made it, where it was from, and what it represented not just emotionally, but also physically. The only other person in this world who knew was Stefania who had been close with my family since we were children. For her the truth needn't explaining, duty was the quintessence of our beings as we both understood that our duties went beyond what we wanted and that for the time we were given we would have to make the most of it. Suddenly, a river of memories with her flashed before my eyes and I was taken back to Christmas Eve of last year. We were just opposite the fireplace, curdled up on the couch drinking hot chocolate and discussing the future looking into the majestic fire burning in the fireplace. The flames were dancing their usual dance ever the sparkling and fierce dancers. That night only missed snow to complete the antithesis with the fire in the fireplace.

I turned to Stefania and said, *"It really isn't Christmas without snow. Snow is a must on Christmas."* She looked at me and as her eyes moved away from mine snow began falling outside the window. As the snow began to thicken her eyes moved away from the window and met mine again suffused with love, care and satisfaction. I can promise you that when two eyes look at you like that you know that this person will be there come rain or shine. Such was our connection that needn't explaining or any attempts at scientific probing. It was simple and genuine, and we were satisfied with where we were at with each other.

A knock on the door shook me back to present time. The maid ran to the door, opened and asked the stylish gentleman standing in front of her who he was. He responded *that he was a close friend and that I was expecting him.* He was absolutely correct in both his statements. It was my good friend Jacob Lawson who had traveled from Paris just to see me, but I was unaware at the time that he had just come for me and not some business as well which was quite uncharacteristic of him to just visit without having any business booked as well. I wasn't complaining though, not a bit since it was extremely difficult to meet true friends and stay in touch let alone meet in person due to how hectic our schedules are. I moved away from the fireplace and ran to the front door. His impeccable dress code was just enough to leave anyone speechless, begging for stylistic advice all the while.

We hugged and with a friendly smile he turned his face to me and placed his hand on my shoulder and said, *"It is so nice to see you again, friend. We haven't seen each other in such a long time. How long has it been? It was four years ago, right?"* He pointed out with a certainty that cancelled out his question.

"Yes, it was almost four years ago," I added.

"I was really looking forward to seeing you today and celebrating your success," He stated with absolute certainty.

How did you? When did he see? I wondered to myself but then I realized, and he just looked at me and with a slight nod he confirmed what I knew all along. He had seen it long before it happened.

"You could have told me sooner that I would successfully close the deal. You would have saved me the trouble of wondering," I said with a slight hint of joyous annoyance in my voice.

Once again, he just looked at me with just a smile on his face and the certainty that we both knew what our conversation was about. My mind began firing at light speed trying to avoid the inevitable result of our conversation. The first thought that popped into my mind was to ask him about the chateau in Bordeaux, which he had recently acquired and was in the process of renovating.

"How are the works at the chateau proceeding," I inquired.

"They have been going strong for about two months to the day. I'm expecting they will finish by the end of the year. We still have much to change. The hard part will be once the works outside have concluded. We'll then have to purchase the antics... You know, now that I think about it, I should move some of the ones I have here in the States to Bordeaux," he appended as if in a legal text.

"I'm so glad everything is moving along nicely..." Before I could finish the sentence, he looked around to make sure no one was within ear shot and his expression darkened.

"You feel it too, don't you?"

"I do. I have had this feeling all day and no matter what it is not going away. Do you think it's *the* sign?" I awkwardly brought my palms together and touched my face while he nodded positively.

"I know the time is nearing when I have to go back, but I need to make sure everything is taken care of here. I have been trying to ensure the smooth sailing of the company and the house for months now."

"My friend, I do believe it's time you went back. I saw the Nebula last night which can only mean one thing. His power is growing, and you might be one of the few people who can stop him. Your parents are really worried about the turn things have taken, and it's high time you pay them a visit and ready yourself for what is to come. I feel his power might start bleeding through this world. There aren't many of us to contain it. You know how He can bend people to his will," he completed his train of thought and in that moment, I realized how right he was and that I had put off my responsibilities for far too long.

"Let the others know that you will be going back, especially Stefania. She deserves to know the whole truth. Tell her the full truth tonight at dinner. She needs to know to be able to protect herself, you and the rest of our community," he interjected.

"I will let her know tonight," I promised.

"I don't think you should delay. I had to eliminate one of his thralls on my way here. Plus, I saw a possible attack on you and Stefania tonight. You know I can't see past this realm, but I'm sure you will be needed soon."

"I trust your sight, my friend. Thank you so much for coming to see me right away," I said reluctantly being flooded with a million possibilities of what I had just heard and what it might mean for my future.

Jacob stood up, grabbed his jacket and started walking towards the exit where the maid was waiting to open the door for him.

Once he reached the door, he stood immobile for a minute as if he was contemplating some deep thoughts;

he turned around, looked into my eyes and said, *"I really hope you succeed. We all depend on you and your leadership in the crisis to come."* I walked with him to his car, he shook my hand and bid me goodbye, but his goodbye felt bitter and final, but I understood what this might mean for me in the future. He had performed his duties as a friend admirably, but now it was my time to do the same since not just one person depended on me. Jacob's visit could only mean that the feeling of dread I had all day was coming true in the realest way possible.

For a moment as his car was speeding away, I felt the weight of responsibility trying to drag me under like a whirlpool from which there was no escape. In the past I had to make multiple sacrifices, leave many behind, focus on my responsibility to protect others, survive away from my family and still manage to thrive despite it all. It was this thought that consoled me and gave me the strength to move forward, to face whatever was thrown at me and possibly emerge victorious. I had to go back and soon. Time seemed was of the utmost importance, though I would still try to have one last night with the one I loved before being forced to part ways.

THE WAY THROUGH

After Jacob's car had vanished from the horizon, I went back into the house and found myself and thoughts racing towards the finish line by attempting to organize them in a succinct fashion that would generate the best course of action. I hared up to my bedroom, crossed the living room of my bedroom in seconds and locked the door behind me.

I extended my right arm and spoke the words, *Noctua veni ad me. Mihi loquere. Nihil retineas.* Once the incantation was finished a dark puff of smoke appeared in front of me only to take the shape of a black owl with black glistening feathers, ruby-red eyes and a tail with sharp feathers that clung together three times. The owl despite its lifelike appearance was nothing but an illusion only a witch could physically touch. Witches have been using them for centuries to communicate with members of their families across dimensions and use them to divine the future. I hadn't used a Noctua in years; I found myself fumbling for words given that Noctuae are extremely dangerous and unreliable in how they produce results given the nature of the questions they are asked. A wrong question or an incomplete one would elicit a similar response. The creature gazed into my eyes to divine the intention behind the question I was about to ask. Before I got to ask the question, the creature flew towards my fireplace and stood majestically on the mantle. Moments later it turned its head acting as if it were scanning the room top to bottom to verify that it was worth its time to provide me with a response regarding the question I was about to ask.

When its eyes met mine, it fixated on me and tilted its head nodding right and left. It had been so long since I had a creature from the other realm in my presence. Its ruby-red eyes were piercing, red like an inferno contained in the body of a tiny creature. I took a couple of minutes before I could muster the strength to ask my question.

"Will my return home aid me in halting the spreading of the Darkness? Will I be able to protect my family?" I asked inquisitively.

"I thought you knew how to ask the right questions, my Lord," the bird voiced its statement with a slight hint of contempt.

"Answer me, creature. I command you to reply to my question. You are fully aware you can't resist replying to any question I ask you," I grudgingly pointed out.

"Such petulance even from one such as you will not be tolerated once you've reached your home realm," the bird replied.

"This is your last chance to do as I ask. You know the power I hold and who I am. Do you really believe it's not in your best interest to conform?" I continued.

"My Lord, I will show you whatever you desire, but I should warn you that this which is contained in any prophecy of fixed future point that our eyes can clearly view cannot be changed completely, altered in any form or fashion. Any attempt may result in cataclysmic events capable of wiping the magical realm off or altering the delicate balance of magic," the bird seemed expressionless and cold similarly to how their species would typically act.

Noctuae are a species of seer-like birds possessing infinite divination powers far more potent than any witch could ever possess on their own hence how even the most powerful witches would consult them to verify their visions. Their nature as neutral beings can generally mean that they could be trusted in their predictions. Personally, I never trusted their visions despite being clearer and this bird seemed much too unwilling to provide me with the information I required despite its initial show of force and swift conversion after I threatened it. Despite this, I had planned for such an eventuality by spelling the vision while active and deciphering any possible nuances at a later time while I was on my way home. I slowly inched towards the table in the middle of the room, I extended my arm, and the bird flew towards me, sat on my arm and requested that I bring my right index to its beak. I did so and its beak bit down on my index drawing three drops of blood that went directly into its mouth. Its eyes flashed a blood-red color while mine suddenly could look beyond the stars and moons, beyond the realms and the afterlife. Our shared vision showed a sweeping Darkness covering the Earth, my family on the brink of death, many of my close friends depowered filled with an overwhelming feeling of powerlessness and despair. The dark figure that haunted this vision appeared at the very end gazing into my mind. Once the vision ended, we both stumbled and almost collapsed from the exhaustion it had caused.

The Noctua had served its purpose. I had the vision and now I could decipher it and look for potential loopholes or anything I might have missed during this initial viewing. With a sweeping motion of my right arm, the seer was gone, and I was left to ponder the possible underlying symbolisms of my vision that would point me to the right direction. The thoughts became raging like a river that flows backwards against the laws of nature. This is what it usually feels like with visions. When you have them, you feel as if your physical body is swept away by a powerful water current, meanwhile your mental body remains immobile in the vision dimension. The tricky thing about visions is that they have numerous interpretations based on how capable the recipient is. The more accomplished you are in this specific branch of magic the more you can see, the more you can decode each time you go back to them.

Despite the inordinate certainty that I was going back home tonight, I was determined to make the best of what little time I had left with Stefania. Once again, my intrinsic motivation and drive to succeed coupled with my unwavering sense of self allowed me to mentally and physically sail past the detrimental sensation of horror that had gripped me tightly minutes earlier. *I was determined to go back, fulfill my duties to my family and country.* I had to suppress all negative feelings for just a few hours, but the how was a tricky subject. It was as tricky as getting the truth from most people in a world where everyone looks out for themselves without ever appreciating the actions and the lengths you have gone to just to help them out in a tough situation. I was most assuredly aware of the shortcomings of humans, but I never truly blamed them for how they are wired simply because I was fully aware that to break free from how you are built is nearly impossible for the majority. It takes courage and the will to change above all before you can truly change. Recognizing where you are and where you want to go are the two requisite steps in the direction of permanent change. Having been in this plane of existence since I was five years old, allowed to experience a different life than the rest of my family, for which I was most thankful. After Jacob's visit, the house didn't feel the same, the world around me didn't feel familiar; a sensation I hadn't felt in almost twenty years. I was only five years old when Stefania and I were brought to this realm. My parents had decided to send us to Earth to safeguard my life until it was time for me to return. It was just me and her for the longest time. As time went by, we began developing feelings for each other and for a while our lives were all about business and the corporate world, but the inevitable return to our home realm never escaped me; not for a moment, really. On the outside it didn't seem like it, but most assuredly you don't forget how your life can change so drastically in moments because of someone else's decisions you have no control over.

Quite honestly, I never blamed my parents. I fully comprehended their reasons. I have to admit that I was kind of relieved when I was brought here, not because I wanted to run from my duties, but because I would get to have the semblance of a life that the rest of my family would never get to experience. Wanting to protect one's child is the primordial force behind any parent's decisions. Thinking back to my early years, I was the most excited to assume my official duties when I came of age, but one night during the Festival of Lights one of the thralls attacked and I was almost killed which prompted the family to sequester me to a place filled with possibility but none of the dangers I would have to face had I stayed. A Thrall is a dark ghostlike creature created by the One-Who-Resides-In-Darkness with multiple abilities capable of wreaking havoc on other magical creatures. If one of them had found its way to Earth, the situation was in fact explosive back home.

Jacob had managed to eliminate it before it got to me, which I imagine it must have taken a great toll on him. His pride wouldn't allow him to tell me, of course. On the other hand, Stefania was to be my protector and friend, but as you already know things had taken a different route. Her full name was Stefania Vitale, a colleague, a lover and one of the Noverfolk. Jacob was also one of the Noverfolk.

You may wonder what a Noverfolk is. They are a special race of humans from Earth born with the innate ability to possess magical abilities which they owe to their ancestry. All of them have one magical parent and can willingly extend their lifetime once every century or so. They owe their creation to the Goddess Cientia, who in her immense wisdom, had given birth to the first of them as a failsafe to protect the Connected Realm from ever been taken over by the Darkness. On Earth, their home realm, they possessed heightened abilities, while my abilities were somehow dampened and couldn't access the full powers I would have in my home realm, which made them the perfect specimen for protectors on Earth. They were warriors, in a way. I knew most of them on Earth, but if what I had seen was to come to pass not even their combined forces could stop the Darkness from taking over the Earth realm.

All the thoughts of what my leaving might mean fired at the speed of light in my head, trying to find an escape and manifest into the physical world. I dismissed them, gathered myself up and decided that I would make the last day on Earth count. I walked past the great clock of the second floor. Time was, indeed, as ruthless as they say. I couldn't believe my eyes. It was 6:04 p.m. I really had to get a move on, get ready, pick a car and head to the restaurant for my date. I rushed to the closet and upon entering the lights turned on. Upon laying my eyes on the masterpiece I had designed; my troubles became a little less for a moment. This house I had designed on my own, it was the first house I ever designed and built. Being a lover of all things classical, the house was designed on the principle of open floor plan, nude shades of paint, straight lines with some hints of rococo here and there. My main bedroom, for example, was one of those rooms drowned in the excessiveness of rococo, exuberant and obnoxiously theatrical, abounding in gold details, classical furniture and a fireplace that would make any head of state or millionaire go green with envy. The closet wasn't an exception. Now that I come to think of it, it must have been the size of a small house. As you entered, on your right-hand side you'd find all kinds of shoes, formal, sportswear, day-to-day, boots, some running shoes and so on. In the middle of the room, I had placed an island-like structure to hold valuable jewelry ranging from watches to tennis bracelets and necklaces, some of which were brought from my realm when we landed here to help me out start my life. On the left-hand side of the closet, all my suits were arranged by color and occasionally I would usually wear them. As my eyes were foraging for the right color and cut, they caught a glimpse of a light blue suit that I was sure would fit the occasion perfectly. I approached the glass door, opened it and carefully retrieved the suit. I set it carefully on the bed as if one would set down a valuable or easily breakable object. Though it may sound as if it were an easy decision, it had taken me about an hour to decide on the right suit to wear.

I headed down the main staircase and called for the housekeeper.

"Gladys, Gladys," I yelled.

"Yes, Mr Aurumstein," she replied almost instantly.

"I want to thank you for your service and patience all this time. You have been a great asset to me in helping me manage my life better on the daily. I'm very pleased I've had you this long," I said thinking I was probably not going to see her any time soon.

Her expression darkened. It was almost as if she was to be fired.

"Are you firing me?" she remarked.

"No, no. God, no," I hurriedly responded. "Far from it! I only wanted to let you know that I'll be moving away for some time. Miss Vitale will be taking over for the time being. I'm leaving on a business trip tonight."

"Thank God you are not firing me. I got scared for a minute there. I will do my best to be of service to her as well," she remarked with a huge smile on her face.

I smiled back and raced past her to quickly gather the rest of my stuff to be put in the car as time was not a friend of mine at the time. Time felt like it was racing past me like a shooting star all day and now that midnight was drawing nearer that feeling was only intensifying. I headed down to the garage, hit the controller and as the doors began rolling up and some of the remaining natural light began to trickle in. An eight-car garage was exposed to the last light Earth would offer me for a long time to come. A deep dark blue Aston Martin DBR1 was my car of choice for that night. It matched my suit, shoes and keys so I thought to myself, *Why not? Seems like the right choice.* I opened the door, got in, started the car, made sure that I had everything I needed and drove out of the driveway towards what would be my last night on Earth. The restaurant was at least half an hour away from my house.

The traffic lights seemed lifeless for the first time in all my years on Earth. The red and green had an unseen melancholy, dimmed brightness as if they knew what was coming. They were withering away like a flower gone without water for weeks. I couldn't help but share their frustration and sadness regarding what was coming. When I reached downtown, hundreds of people were crossing the streets, some were in their cars heading to their favorite club, bar or restaurant, others were shopping while others were running the final errands of the day. While stopped at an intersection, I looked to my right automatically. A man was banging his head against an ATM, a few feet away two young women were walking their dogs calmly and had their heads buried in their phones, a couple in the car on my left was loudly arguing about some work stuff while the children in the back were crying. It was in that moment I came to the realization I would miss this chaotic and emotion-driven world.

The light turned green, I pressed the gas pedal lightly and made a left turn, looked at the dashboard and realized it was already 8:24 p.m. *You still have time. Don't worry. The traffic isn't so terrible,* I thought to myself. The restaurant was at least ten minutes away. I still don't remember how many buildings and people I had driven past by the time I got to the restaurant. The city seemed and felt abuzz with life and light despite the recurring feeling that the world was changing around me as the time for my departure was drawing nearer by the minute. I finally got to the restaurant and much to my surprise a parking spot was available. The valet of the restaurant approached me and as I was rolling down the window, I heard him comment under his breath, *"My man, this car is bitching. Nice wheels, dude."* He was so sure I hadn't heard him, but my smile betrayed me. His face changed to that of a child that was about to get scolded for commenting inappropriately and unprofessionally in the place of work.

"It's OK. Don't sweat it," I assured him.

"Thank you, sir. It was unprofessional of me to say that," he admitted and lowered him head.

"It's totally fine," I reassured him. Take good care of the car and no joy rides until I come back," I jokingly remarked.

"I wouldn't dream of it," he admitted to me knowing full well he would lose his job if he did so.

As soon as I turned my head, across the street Stefania had just parked her car in a free spot and was exiting her car. You can't imagine what this woman meant to me, her beauty was only surpassed by her intelligence and gentle spirit. That night was perhaps the most beautiful I had seen her. Her raven hair was caressing her shoulders like a feather caresses the wind. Even from a distance, her hair glowed complimenting the red dress she had on and the white fur that had covered the back of her dress. It didn't take her long to perceive me. She looked across the street and smiled at me as though we hadn't seen each other in years. Her heartwarming smile was met with one of my own in reciprocity, but that warm feeling was soon to be replaced with a feeling of horror as a dark figure began to appear behind her. My eyes couldn't believe that a thrall would dare attack someone in the open especially a protector like her.

"Look out! A thrall!" I yelled at her in a mental message that reached her mind in milliseconds.

She seemed calm and collected despite the imminent danger. I hadn't seen one of their kind in twenty years. Her hair pulled itself up, she turned around and with a violent slap-like hand movement she suspended the creature mid-air in a telekinetic grip it couldn't escape from. She snapped her fingers, and an invisibility spell cloaked her from the eyes of the people passing by. I rushed to her faster than a bullet. The thrall was trying desperately to escape her grip, but to no avail. Its eyes were darker than the blackest night, its body wrapped in shadow, writhing in a manner so violent it was as if we were witnessing the death of a star. In desperation it started chanting a *breaking enchantment,* but thankfully I remembered the counter spell from my childhood. It was so long since I cast a proper spell, I had almost forgotten the feeling of power as the words left my mouth. Once the spell was completed, the thrall was rendered speechless, therefore completely powerless to act on its orders and urges.

"It's the second one this week," Stefania remarked.

"You mean you were attacked again, and you didn't tell me?" I yelled.

"This is neither the time nor the place to talk about this. I'm a bit preoccupied right now." She was, in fact, intently focusing on the spell otherwise the creature would escape her.

With her free hand, she opened the Fourth Portal that would take me directly to my family. I wasn't going to leave her like this nor was I going to allow her to not join me.

"Go, Bormia will be waiting on the other side of that portal. She has already been made aware of what's happening," she exclaimed. She telekinetically hurled me through the portal before I had the chance to act.

"No!" I shrieked as the portal was closing behind me. My mind began to race with my first thought being how she would fare against the thrall alone.

SELTRA

As I went through the portal, my mind began to flare up unable to reconcile what had just happened with what was about to come. Though the portal didn't take long to get me to my destination it felt like an entire lifetime. Once the portal to Seltra closed behind me, I immediately began to feel the rush of power that came with being in my home realm. Seltra was the magical dimension that existed parallel to the human realm of Earth. I, on the other hand, being a royal descendant and being in my home realm afforded me great strength in magic and in physical terms. *I hadn't gone through a portal in almost twenty years.* The sensation was otherworldly, eerie even. In my home world, such means of transportation are usually employed to traverse through great distances and dimensions without being forced to occupy the space in between. Much to my surprise, the portal landed me at the edge of the gilded forest, quite clumsily I should say. As I stood on my feet, my eyes filled with nostalgia and awe of the beauty of the world I had left behind two decades ago, my eyes allowed a tiny teardrop to fall down my right chick.

The Gilded Forest was one of my grandmother's creations as a means of additional protection for our family seeing as it covered the Royal Palace in a shroud of impenetrable magic. I remember the story she used to tell me to this day; she planted a gold seed of the Ancient Trees she had in her possession since her childhood, a gift from her own mother. Once she planted the Original Seed the entirety of the forest grew around it in just under a day. It was the time of the great invasion when my family was tasked with defending the realm and the royal palace. The great battle against the Dark Emperor was fought on this very ground with my grandmother spearheading the attack. When I was a child, many in the royal court and outside of it used to talk of my grandmother's bravery in battle and, of course, her immense magical skills no one should underestimate. Once the battle was over, the battle ground was soaked with the blood of the enemies of Seltra. On this battle ground, the Seed was planted. The gilded trees around me were so lively, so lifelike as if they were ready to talk to me, to greet me in their own way. The path I was standing on comprised barely of any visible grass. The gold flaked grass created an optical illusion unlike anyone would expect to see in their lifetime. As I walked down the path, the trees bent over to greet me, extended their branches and leaves to touch me and whisper in my ears. The gilded trees were bejeweled with more than just gold, rubies, emeralds, silver and many more precious stones covering their barks and branches.

For a moment there I forgot that I was supposed to meet Bormia where the portal landed me. Bormia was an old friend and court member I hadn't spoken to since I left.

"A court member?" I muttered under my breath. She was much more than just a court member. The position she held in the Royal Court was one that inspired envy, awe and fear and stirred unease in the hearts of many. Bormia along with her sisters Melona, Isira and Ferna were known as the four in one, an extremely rare race of witches known as the Quattuor. The power of the Quattuor was discovered by my distant ancestors when they traversed on a royal visit to the island of Bernol almost 400 hundred years ago. The royal family of Bernol has been close friends and allies since the Great War and I imagined that to this day such a strong bond wouldn't have been severed no matter what in all my years of absence. I had visited the island last when I was just four years old, on a royal visit with my parents and siblings. To this day, I will never forget the beauty of that island, cascading waters, wonderful people, and a palace that would put many of the others in the realm to shame. The queen and king of Bernol were gracious hosts from what I could remember. Their children and courtesans were similar in temperament. On the balcony of the great hall, many had gathered to witness our visit while our Quattuor stood guard on

either side of our families that day. The sun was glistening above us, the waters surrounding the island would dance at our arrival even the animals would flock to our gathering. I will never consign to oblivion the last day of our visit. The stable hand under orders of the king led me to the stables and presented me with a Pegasus, a winged warhorse, which took a liking me to me instantly.

My grandmother had told me the story about how the Quattuor came to serve in our royal court. Her great-grandmother had discovered their unique abilities and magical prowess which would further benefit our House. The former Queen at the time had agreed to part with her guard as a gift to the Empress, which she accepted and vowed to take care of them and ensure the continuation of their line. The Quattuor possessed powers like no one had ever seen in Seltra. Their powers could match gods and Higher Beings. One of their most striking features was their black hair, unison in responses and the ability to link their magic as well as copy and contain the powers of even a goddess as powerful as Cientia.

My reminiscing ended abruptly when a familiar voice sounded in the distance.

"Your Royal Highness, it is such an honor to welcome you back home. We have missed you in court." Bormia smiled with such a glow emanating from her beaming smile.

"Hi, old friend. I have missed all of you so dearly," I admitted to her and myself if I were completely honest.

"Let's take you back. Everyone is waiting for you in the throne room."

We moved past the last trees and a carriage was waiting at the end of the road exiting the forest. Such a regal carriage, coated in precious stones and the family crest. I was beyond moved, at a loss for words examining every little detail of the world I had left behind all those years ago. In the front of the carriage, four majestic horses were ready to haul us to the palace. Along the way, the scenery never ceased to fail to arouse the interest of any traveler passing through those lands. Bormia remained silent for most of the way, contemplating how she should act around me given how we parted ways at the tender age of five. The interior of the carriage was lush; red silk cushions, additional pillows with the family crest embroidered on top of all of them, the curtains were of similar color and flowed downwards in a seamless manner. On the outside, the carriage seemed to be of average length, but once you stepped inside it extended via the use of a spell to *extend the space within.* The dominant color was a crimson red, howbeit some royal blues and greens broke up the monotony of red. Bormia was sitting right across from me dressed in the traditional state wear of the Quattuor. The crimson red dress she wore matched fully the surrounding coach interior, on either hand she bore the royal rings that held extra power gathered from her sisters in case we stumbled upon any trouble on the way home.

The coachmen were stationed in the front of the carriage and the back as well, while two guards were marching on their horses on either side of the carriage inspecting the road ahead to make sure no one was following us. Bormia's eyes suddenly flashed a crimson-red color, she tapped the roof of the carriage three times; an indication that we had arrived, which was a sign I clearly missed the first couple of seconds. *I had been gone for a long time.* I hurriedly pulled the curtains open only to see that my arrival was met with excitement and full attendance from all courtesans and commoners from surrounding villages. I opened the door, stood frozen for a minute as if I had been transformed into a statue and then the people in attendance cheered, yelled and welcomed me with such warmth and tenderness I hadn't experienced in a long time.

As I dismounted the carriage, a child grabbed my hand out of nowhere; I turned to my right and bent down to greet my young subject.

"Thank you for coming back, Your Highness. We need your help. My dad is missing. Can you help us?" The boy's words sounded genuinely filled with pain and despair. I had no idea what he meant by *missing,* but given how I had been hearing rumors about the Obsidian Emperor returning it wasn't far-fetched that his claim would be true. I nodded positively to the child

and his eyes brightened with joy and hope. In seconds, a guard had approached and attempted to remove the child from my presence to which I responded discreetly by simply waving at him to stay back and never attempt anything like this when I was conversing with a subject. He froze in place and averted his gaze pretending to not have acted in a certain unwanted manner. Perhaps, he had forgotten how we, as royals had to be close to the people and allow them to voice their concerns and complaints in a respectful manner. Judging by how I was met upon arrival, I could discern that my parents' rule had remained successful under my grandmother's tutelage.

When I was but a child, my duties involved being among the people, with my siblings by my side at all times while under heavy guard and sometimes accompanied by our grandmother. My memories were inextricably connected to my grandmother and siblings; memories I cherished and held with me while on Earth. I would now have to set my Earth memories aside and focus on the tasks ahead. While all subjects were cheering my arrival, I was led into the palace through the main door with Bormia constantly by my side. With a single move of her hand, the gigantic doors of the throne room swung open. The throne room was a thing of beauty, a marvel of architecture, an amalgamation of white marble and gold details with hidden hints of silver. The doors were made of pure gold with two humungous handles that needed two people to open should magic not be an option. The floors of the massive throne room had marble covering every inch of the room from beginning to end. *I'm back.* It must have been one sentence I repeated to myself even I don't know how many times, all sounds became muffled for a split second as I breathed in the crystal clear air that filled the room. The ceiling was so far away it was almost impossible to distinguish where it ended. An enchantment had been cast and the ceiling rained rose petals to celebrate my arrival in traditional Seltran fashion. The columns supporting the room were also made up of marble with infinite gold details embossed all around them, while the walls in the distance had murals detailing the history of our nation, ranging from how we had come to be to recent history. The beauty of this building was beyond any human or magical languages can describe.

There must have been thousands of nobles in attendance, nobles from all across the dimension. I remember seeing Seltran nobles, pixie envoys, pixie royals, high-ranking witches from the Kingdom of the Mountains, our distant relatives and species I hadn't seen since my childhood. As I walked towards the thrones, in the distance, my parents stood perched upon their golden thrones, my brother and sister on either side of them, while my grandmother sat comfortably right in the middle. Suddenly silence fell across the room as the royal herald began to make his announcements.

"Today, it is a joyous occasion for all of us. Our firstborn prince, the future king of Seltra has finally been repatriated. Join us in the celebrations to come. Such is the nature of hard times. Allies come together, enemies lurk in the shadows aiming to strip us of our freedom, but our history shows that we are strong enough to resist the seduction of dark and carve our own path and protect our lands," the herald assured the other royals in attendance.

His words filled me with hope and strength for I truly had no idea what was to come. Not one bit. I mean I had a slight inkling of what I would have to face, but things took a turn for the worst almost immediately after my arrival. It was as if I was destined to never find peace, like the feeling you have when you feel absolutely and unapologetically happy, but this feeling comes to an abrupt end once the other shoe drops. It was exactly this feeling I began to feel here. *The other shoe will drop. This seems too good to be true.* I felt the constricting grip of destiny around my throat holding me down like a tortured soul about to be led by the psycho pomp to the gates of the afterlife. No matter what, there was no internal conflict in me. I had to make it; I had to succeed in the mission I felt was coming my way. I was sure I would hear about it sooner rather than later. For now I would enjoy the meal and reconnecting with my family, but tomorrow my true work wouldbegin. The king and queen had announced the preparation of the royal feast in their invitations and now the herald was officially announcing it, too. During the first celebration of the day I didn't get the chance to talk to my siblings or my parents. Our only greetings were only exchanged mentally throughout the ceremony. After the end of the official proceedings, the herald invited our guests to head to the royal dining hall. We would join everyone about an hour later after we had properly reconnected in private. Bormia led me into my old room where I would have to stoically await my siblings. She closed the door, sealed it with a spell as a precaution given how dangerous it had become living in the kingdom. It was then that I fully realized that it was, indeed, a different home to the one I remembered. However, I didn't have to wait long until my brother and sister rushed into the room. When they were outside, I immediately felt the shield Bormia had put crumble of its own volition since it was meant to keep everyone else out apart from my brother and sister. They came running into the room and launched themselves into my hug. It felt as though I was being hugged by an avalanche. Such was the love we had for each other, but also the reason we had to part ways all those years ago.

"Brother, you have to tell us everything," Aurora said.

"How is Earth?" Cornelius inquired.

"We have missed you so much around here. You have no idea how difficult it has been without our brother around," she continued.

"The situation is critical, but tonight we are to celebrate our brother," he cut her off.

I knew she was going to expand on this, but I was way too happy to see both of them. I felt an immense feeling of pride because I hadn't forgotten how to read my sister. She was the version of me on Earth; all about business, the grind and responsibility. *I was truly gone for a long time. I had missed so many of their birthdays, celebrations, problems, long, late hours catching up.* We used to talk and spend time with each other since we were born. This is something we would do as children even as toddlers. Our bond was unbreakable with both my siblings. My brother was the one less likely to open up as fast, unlike my sister, but I was just glad to have them in my presence again. I will never forget the birth of my sister. Such a beautiful baby she was. Shining with potential and gifts long before she was even born and now, she was a proper woman in every way. My brother's birth was under different circumstances, however. Not as lucky as my sister. He was born right at the ending of a battle where our mother had led our troops into victory, a fact which only adds to the importance and resilience of Seltran women, royal or commoner. He, too, had changed a lot like my sister. In that moment nothing else mattered other than how I felt to have both my brother and sister with me.

"How has Grandmother been?" I asked without realizing the full scope of how Seltra had changed in my absence.

My brother's expression darkened as if he had just witnessed something gruesome. I saw him trying to find the right words in his mind before voicing any thoughts out loud.

"Speak!" I yelled.

My voice raised as if I was talking to someone who had just angered me beyond reason, but it was truly anxiety that seized me; anxiety coupled with worry. My sister stepped in to assuage my anger and calm my tension by placing her hand on my shoulder.

"Grandmother has been different of late. The Obsidian Emperor's power is beginning to bleed into this world from his fortress of Shadow and I think it's affecting her somehow due to the Forest Protection. Do you remember that it was a battlefield before the forest was created by her?" she reminded me.

"Of course, I remember," I replied.

"I have been feeling some disturbances coming from the forest even though her magic shields the entirety of the forest, the blood of the fallen thralls must still be under the roots of some trees which affects the integrity of the spell she cast all those decades ago. You know that she elected me to be the next one to take on the task of holding down the dark forces by reinforcing the spell on my coronation day," she explained.

I was horrified at what my ears had just heard, but I had decided to not allow bad tidings ruin what was possibly the last peaceful night we would ever have in a long while.

"Tonight we celebrate, but tomorrow our real work begins," I tried wording in the calmest manner I could muster.

"I'm sorry, brother. It's just that I had been apart from you both and our parents and my mind immediately went to something terrible," I revealed.

"I fully understand, brother," Cornelius responded in a saddened manner.

"Now, let's make our way to the feast and tomorrow we will strategize on how to defend ourselves and the kingdom."

Bormia opened the door, and as we exited she sealed my room again without wasting any time and along with two guards, she accompanied us out to the great dining hall. Either side of the corridor we were going through hosted the paintings of our ancestors, politically and historically significant individuals, allies from the past as well as enemies who had been defeated by our forces throughout our long history. The paintings on the walls were not just lifeless pieces of arts, but rather a living embodiment of the past, present and future. Many bowed their heads in respect as we went past them. Imagine never truly losing your ancestors and always having access to their wisdom even after they had left their immortal coil. A detail of substantial significance is that though witches are considered immortal, they can be killed if the right conditions are met. Royal witches, however, have numerous immunities to the common weaknesses other witches possess. If you stick with me to the end of the story, you will get to know and experience the tragic end and beginning of our life chapters. For now, the feast in the great hall awaited our arrival. I wasn't planning to disappoint. That night my siblings and I had to put on the performance of a lifetime.

UNLIKELY ALLIES

The door of the dining hall unlocked, unbolted and the scrumptious feast had already begun despite our absence. The two guards directed us to our seats, pulled the chairs and waited until we were seated to step back. I was seated next to my mother on her right, whereas my siblings were seated on the left side next to our father. Many magical races were in attendance; they had traversed from different countries to join us in the Feast of feasts which is usually thrown when a new royal is soon to take the reins or even celebrate the return of one. Our table was placed at the end of the room as you entered it so that everyone in attendance could have an unobstructed view of the royal members. The queen sat at the head of the table as is customary for a reigning monarch to do, a queen regnant in her case. Our mother had inherited the throne from her mother, who was the previous monarch. However, the queen's mother had remained an important aspect of royal life maintaining her position in court as the Queen Mother. To us she was simply Grandma or Grandmother, but to the rest of the world she was the Queen Mother Eutychia, a descendant of the great kings and queens of Old. Her daughter was Queen Millia, who married early in life –

it was an arranged marriage – but they had come to care for one another and their children and subjects. King Infinitus, upon marriage became the king consort of Seltra. As king and queen they were loved by the people due to how they would always care and preoccupy themselves with the problems of the common folk believing that their subjects' problems were their problems as well. Aside from king and queen, they were also known as emperor and empress having ruled over the vast and endless realms of the kingdom of Seltra and other adjacent realms. The Earth was bequeathed to my mother from her own mother as the dimension where the only magical beings to exist would be the Noverfolk. During the feast, I believe I had conversed with almost every major noble and royal from across the realm discussing their concerns, inquiries and anything that they would deem as important or discussion worthy. I have to admit that I wasn't bored or disheartened by the amount of complaints I had heard, not in the slightest.

The king and queen seemed to be enjoying their feast despite the heavy sense of doom everyone felt but no one voiced at any point during the first half of the feast. They, too, had conversed with an inordinate amount of nobles throughout the feast, but when Prince Solner approached, I felt a slight tingle of embarrassment; I hadn't even noticed my father's brother, Crown Prince Solner.

"Uncle!" I yelled. "I just noticed you. I hope you don't begrudge me this slight oversight. I don't even know how many I have talked to," I said apologetically.

"Do not feel embarrassed, nephew. I'm simply glad to have you back safe and sound. I have heard all about what happened on Earth. I hope Stefania beat the devil chasing you both, but in any case, she is expendable."

"Uncle, I love Stefania. We have been together for years and I would appreciate it if you talked better about her. She is not a thing to be considered expendable," I remarked angrily.

"Nephew, we do not befriend or bed the Noverfolk. They serve a purpose; a purpose of protection to us real magical beings, nothing more nothing less. I don't mean to lessen your feelings for her, and I hope you understand where I come from. I don't mean to bring you down," he replied trying to cover up his obvious lack of knowledge on the matter.

"Uncle, let me be very clear about some things. I will be the reigning monarch soon enough and you should remember your place in this court. I pray you understand what I mean and remain cautious in your wording from this point forward," I carefully outlined.

During my discussion with my uncle and his subsequent leaving my sight, I had not neglected to observe that one of the vampire princes of the northern kingdom had been eavesdropping on my private conversation to which I responded by angrily staring at him. It was prince Laur, the next in line for the northern kingdom throne. His father and mine had been friends for decades, but we were a different story. When I was younger, we were good friends and he would come to visit us many times over, but one specific point in time changed everything between us; a happening so heart-wrenching for me that I wouldn't even care to expand on. Vampires had always been one of my most beloved creations of the goddess, many of whom I had befriended in the past and many of whom I had defended on multiple occasions. *I love vampires so much.* The moment I realized I was to come back home the vampires were the one race I was really looking forward to meeting with after having reconnected with my family. Such was their fierce beauty and temperament that even Laur was irresistible to me though, his hypnotic powers would not work on someone as strong as me in magic. Vampires were creatures of immense beauty, ethereal elegance and possessed powers that terrified many, even when hearing them being talked about without them being physically present. Their tall build would intimidate many and leave nothing to the imagination regarding how effective and lethal they could be in battle.

Unlike their Earth counterparts, no such weaknesses were part of their actual mythology. No crosses could harm them, garlic wouldn't repel them in any form or fashion, nor would they be permanently killed should their hearts get damaged. Fire didn't pack much damage to their bodies. The only way to effectively kill them would be to destroy their creator or untangle their sire line, but Laur had no such weaknesses due to him being descended from true vampires, and also being born and not made. Their physical beauty was almost unmatched, their usual charisma unparalleled. Amongst the many species of the realm of Seltra they were by far the tallest and most physically powerful. Some of them would become even more powerful by learning to harness magic and use to their advantage in battle. Laur was the perfect specimen of their kind. He possessed all their common traits, almost none of their weaknesses and on top of that he had learned to harness some forms of magic. It was also said that he was able to summon the Old Powers with which he would threaten the Obsidian Emperor during the last battle that determined and sealed the fate of Seltra and all the realms of the magic dimension.

My stare and side-eye was enough to put him in his place and join his faction until the inevitable happened. His companions shared some of his physical traits, which made them insanely attractive to anyone with eyes; an observation I would come to know as very true. I returned back to the royal table, sat at my predetermined post and awaited the fairy envoy to approach the rest of the family to voice the concerns of their people in this time of need. The fairy envoy was an old man dressed in their traditional colors. He approached the table, bowed his head and requested a private audience with me as the next reigning monarch.

I assured him he would be heard and that I would do my absolute best to serve his people the best way I knew how. He initially requested that I visit their country to inspect the troubles the thralls of the Obsidian Emperor had caused to which I responded positively straight away given the nature my trip would take on after I left the palace with my company to head to the Obsidian Gate and destroy the emperor by any means necessary. My words filled him with hope and glee, and he informed me that our agreement would surely reach the ears of the Fairy King and that the king has granted him the right to seal this deal on his behalf. Once we had concluded our business, he bowed respectfully and went back to the table to join the rest of his kind—yet another race that represented the allure and charm of the magical world. Fairies, though beautiful and seemingly frail they were anything but that in reality. Much you would underestimate a child some might have been tempted to do the same with them. Their apparent frailty was nothing short of how they wanted to present themselves to the rest of the world.

Once their magical strength was witnessed by anyone, they would immediately drop any such childish notions. Those in attendance wore elegant dresses of light green, white and silver shades; their wings protruded from their back and almost reached the floor. All of them seemed to be enjoying the scrumptious feast and delicate desserts our chefs had created for them much to my excitement and approval. Though they had been friends of the royal families across the dimension, they had a major disadvantage in my opinion. Fairies tended to be indecisive and avoid conflict which would create practical problems when their allegiance was required by their allies. The only way you could get them to budge was to remind them that if the world was to be left to its fate, without its protectors, the spreading darkness would cover their lands soon thereafter and extinguish their light as well. The same principle applied to their cousins as well; the Pixies were the most indifferent creatures when it came to waror open confrontation. Throughout my discussions with almost everyone that night I had come to the realization that I would have to go to extreme lengths to convince them to join our cause without much dismay or resistance. Before the final battle was to commence, they gave in and acted upon their better instincts, or should I say their better interests. I was thankful for their help since their help was enough to turn the tide of war and tip the balance in our favor. *I was truly thankful for their aid.*

What transpired after I had concluded the discussions with all the factions I didn't expect, but it was the event that set in motion the forging of new alliances and the formation of the company against the Obsidian Emperor. The night drew to its expected end, when all attendees would have to abandon the premises and the Quattuor would magically seal the palace for everyone's safety. Some of the guests would, however, remain under the protection of our roof based on their status as foreign envoys, distant family members as well as cousins and close friends all of whom had been vetted for dark magic before they had entered the palace upon their arrival. The dining hall was almost emptied. Only a select few guests remaining at the time.

In a trice, an intemperate burst of obsidian energy appeared in the middle of the room. The surge of darkness I felt was heart-gripping, it was as though one's heart was being squeezed to death from inside their chest. My breath tightened; my eyes fixated on the darkness to make sure no one would get harmed by him. His coming to the Royal Palace could only have meant one thing for me. The border guards had failed to successfully contain the darkness which had allowed him to escape. The very being that had been responsible for me not having seen my family in twenty years was standing right in front of me. The Obsidian Emperor himself had broken through the outer defenses of the Golden Forest and managed to sneak onto the grounds of the palace. He couldn't have attached himself to one of our guests. *That would have been impossible.* The Quattuor were far too powerful to be tricked by any sort of trickery or deceit even if he had tried to. I knew I couldn't openly confront him or attempt an attack without risking hurting someone close to me. My siblings rushed to my side in case we needed to link and join our powers together to stop him even temporarily. The Emperor was the wielder of massive powers both in physical and magical terms, but aside from his magical prowess he possessed two gifts that made most of the magical community tremble at the mention of even his name. His charisma alone was enough to turn reasonably powerful beings into thralls, infect them with his darkness and the second being his ability to pierce through the veil invading the dream world of almost anyone through which he would manipulate them to the point of madness. His voice would become unbearable in their minds until they would willingly turn to quiet the voices. His army, at the time was growing exponentially, but we would soon come to know the depth of the damage his mere appearance would cause to the kingdom.

His underlings in the shadow dimensions were known to us as the Obsidian Nobles, a race of dark, corrupted witches who had undertaken the responsibility to teach his thralls how to harness their new powers once they had turned. Even though they were significantly less powerful than him, they were not to be underestimated for their powers combined could bring down entire dimensions. Their magic was elemental in nature, for the most part, though they possessed an array of dark spells which they could utilize to achieve a myriad of effects. In the final battle, they were his front line of defense. Their most dangerous trait yet was the fact that they were born witches and not created ones which made their powers all the more potent.

By the time the shadow energy had calmed, everyone in the room had assumed battle positions ready to defend their lives, kingdoms and families. He didn't seem too interested in them, but rather he seemed to barely acknowledge their presence. His eyes were fixated on me and for a few minutes he scanned me up and down as if he was sizing me up to see how much of a threat I would be as one of the potential people in the magical world capable of destroying him completely. He knew of the prophecy at the time, he seemed. A prophecy, the Oracle had previous presented to my mother when I was but a babe months after my birth. I never forgot the words myself. It was as if they had been engraved in my mind, passively stored in my memory.

The Dark will meet its destruction when the firstborn son of Seltra will come of age and power on the day he assumes the throne. The Dark will meet its end on the battlefield of its choosing. The hero of Seltra will sacrifice his life to save the kingdom from total destruction.

Not a very abstract prophecy, I should say, unlike those you usually hear in movies and books. The Oracle was clear and specific about what would have to be done. That was the price to be paid, but as inventive as I am I would have to find a way to work through even a solid prophecy such as this one. That's what I usually told myself. I had always found a way around things in the past. This time I would have to do the same for the people I loved or so I had hoped.

"Aurelius of Seltra," the Dark Emperor shrieked in a foul voice. "Come meet your end at my hands. You have evaded your fate for much too long."

"If you think I will be meeting my end any time soon, you are sadly mistaken," I retorted confidently. "If you think I'm afraid of you, you have seriously underestimated me and my family."

The Quattuor remained motionless never breaking their protection spell.

"Maybe I should kill one of your siblings. Your weakling brother or maybe your pathetic sister," he continued.

"Bring it on! I will be sending you a gift before you draw your final breath, foul fiend," my sister replied with a confidence befitting a Princess.

She didn't seem fazed by his threats and belittling manner neither was my brother who simply scoffed at his comment without paying much mind to it. For the first time maybe in his ageless life he felt that the end was nearing and maybe felt a slight twinge of fear in his cold heart as the only thing he feared was losing his power.

"Come to the Border Country in four days' time. I would love to unleash an attack and destroy everything and everyone, but that would not be any fun," he added in a childish manner. "I know this is when your power will be at its peak. I don't like to fight weak-minded worms."

"I'll be there!" I retorted in the snidest way I could master.

In a similarly violent way in which he had appeared initially, he disappeared. I felt the frustration of everyone in the room as they realized what had just transpired signified the beginning of the end of me and many of them. Laur with whom I hadn't spoken in years, sped to my side as I left the room and just barely caught up to me before I had entered my sealed and magically impenetrable bed chambers. His hand extended and touched my shoulder to which I reacted aggressively.

"Keep your hands off me. Never touch me again or I will trap you in your own mind for eternity."

I really couldn't contain my anger and rage. I had considered him a friend, but he had betrayed my trust in the worst way possible and that was something I couldn't abide by.

"Please, listen to me," he begged. "I have a way to defeat him. It's in my father's possession. The Sword of Creation can pierce his armor and end him once and for all."

His words made sense, but I couldn't trust his word or his ability to lie convincingly. I would have to see for myself. Without any warning, I clenched my right arm and peered into his mind. It was a literal maze from all the centuries of thoughts, but I could discern the parts I wanted to see easily. *He was telling me the truth.* I could hardly believe it.

"You're telling me the truth," I interposed.

"Of course, I'm telling you the truth. We were friends once and I would like us to be again. I can't apologize enough for what happened in the past, but just know that I have missed your friendship all this time you were away," he asserted.

"We will see. Once I have defeated the Obsidian Emperor, we'll—"

"No, you can't do it alone—" he cut me off abruptly.

"I can and I will," I interjected.

His face had really softened since the feast had started and I could sense he was telling me the truth but how could I put my faith in someone who had so easily betrayed me in the past without a serious reason. *I honestly wasn't willing to risk it.* Using his enhanced speed, he reached the end of the hall in less than three seconds, he stood there for a couple more seconds, looked back at me with a face that was more similar to that of a crying child rather than a proud prince and disappeared into the night without uttering a single word. Our paths though would cross again not long after but for the time being I had to think and come up with a plan to defeat the Emperor and his armies, fulfill the prophecy and find a way to move forward after the battle was over. I entered my room and Isira put up the shielding spell that had so graciously and effectively protected me so many times in the past.

An explosion was heard outside my window, I rushed to it and witnessed with my own eyes the darkness spreading from the shadow dimension, but something seemed to be holding it back, something powerful and indiscernible from the great distance. It seemed to be a magical source from the north. I couldn't possibly know who or what that was until I got to the Border Country. I frantically started to prepare for my departure when the idea flashed like a light bulb. The first part of the prophecy was fulfilled. The Emperor had chosen the battlefield where his doom would be decided.

A loud banging on the door cut me off from my thoughts. My siblings were standing right outside my door demanding to be allowed in. Isira dropped the shield with a snap of her fingers after she just had turned her head in my direction to wait for my instructions. Just a nod was enough. The shield was dropped instantaneously. My siblings barged in like a windstorm ready to level anything in its path.

"You can't go! You are not going alone!" they screamed in unison.

"I can. I will and I am going," I replied all the while packing the essentials for my departure.

"If you go alone, we want to be with you mentally. Let us link mentally so that we can give you the requisite strength when the time comes. I will be able to guide you through some of the situations you will encounter along the way," she assured me.

"How do you know what I'm going to encounter?" I inquired.

"I have seen every possible outcome. In your absence I honed my foretelling skills, but I can't see past the dark dimension. The Fairies, Pixies and Vampires will help you in the end. Go to the Sirens first; they have the buxus, the containment box for all magic and the vampires have guarded the Sword of Creation for a century. Laur will be there, too," she fully explained seemingly sure of her predictions.

We joined hands and activated the link between our life forces just in case things got wild in the dark dimension. My siblings seemed too sure of what the outcome would come to be. I wasn't equally optimistic, but I wouldn't want to disappoint them. With a snap of my fingers I had left my bed chamber.

ONWARD TO THE END

My power had brought me to the Siren Cove. I was standing at the entrance of the Cove while remaining linked to my brother and sister to aid me in this arduous four-day journey I had to complete. Through the link they could not only perceive my thoughts but also see through my eyes and speak through my mouth should they need to. Such a feat could only be accomplished with my consent. Thankfully, my sister, Aurora, was extremely knowledgeable in other species' habits, politics, physiologies, and powers. Sirens are creatures of pure arrogance basing their superiority belief system on their external beauty and powerful physiologies. Their pride was only matched by their power; immortal creatures of incalculable powers and abilities ever balancing between good and evil. Their concession in parting with the containment box would solely depend on how I would handle the communication with their queen. The queen was a creature that was hundreds of centuries old who had seen the coming and going of numerous monarchs throughout the decades and centuries. Someone from Earth would recognize them as the mythical creatures of Greek and Roman legends. Sirens lived underwater, but they could easily shed their tails in seconds to walk on land and fight much to the dismay of many of their enemies, who would initially have thought they had an advantage over them.

They were easy to turn the outcome around pretty quickly and smother any indication of rebellion or resistance against them. The Siren society had a very strict hierarchical structure which prevented them from acting according to their own free will, however I felt like I could somehow exploit their inability to lie directly. It goes without saying that this meant that they could shape the truth indirectly by providing half-truths. It took me almost a day to wrap up business with them, but while conversing with the queen I never lost sight of the mission at hand. Once I landed at the entrance, two spear-wielding males arose from the water to greet and bring me before the queen. One of them extended his arm and offered me a seaweed-like plant which I would have to consume in order to be able to travel underwater and retain all my senses. I consumed it right away, my body changed rapidly, and I joined them in their underwater palace. The sea floor was majestic, sublime filled with all manners of plant and sea life. Unfortunately, I couldn't enjoy such a spectacle due to pressing concerns and a limited time frame. In the distance, the palace's torrents peeked above the underwater caverns and mountains. Four turrets stood on either side of the palace around which torrents of living water spun in a seemingly destructive fashion. Sirens were stationed at every gate on the orders of the queen who had probably heard of the arrival of the Emperor, which was a positive indication for me that I might succeed in swaying her to my side.

The guards aggressively stared at me as I was swimming past them to reach the main gate as if I were the enemy. I hadn't seen their kind act so unfriendly towards someone like me especially given how our species and kingdoms had been the best of friends and on the best of terms for centuries. Inside the palace the situation wasn't any different, but the queen I met with in the throne room seemed more amenable than her subjects. Upon entering any open space within the palace, the water on the other side was alive, even sentient one might say, and from the side of the ocean no water whatsoever, nowhere to be found. There was breathable air and the Sirens inside the palace had no need for their aquatic form. The guards led me to the throne room where the queen was surrounded by her war council discussing possible options regarding the return of the Obsidian Emperor. One of their guards who had led me to the palace from the surface interrupted her midsentence by clearing his throat loudly to which she didn't take very calmly deeming his action as unacceptable.

"How dare you interrupt your Queen?" she yelled at him. "Leave my sight now!"

She then turned to me only to welcome me in the warmest way her race could master.

"Welcome, Your Highness. I've been expecting your arrival for a couple of days now," she added.

"Thank you for having me on such short notice. Could we discuss some matters of urgency in private?" I demanded calmly.

"Leave us," she ordered her council.

The council didn't seem all too happy to abide by her command. I could sense the mistrust in their eyes. *I thought Sirens possessed the skill of deduction or better yet reasoning.* Maybe something had happened that had forced them to withdraw from their allies and friends. I was *not* the enemy. That much I knew. Now, I had figure out the *why*.

"Excuse them, Aurelius. They honestly don't mean to be unfriendly, especially after all this time that our kingdoms have been friends."

"I'm guessing something has happened recently that would force you to double your guards along the borders. What was it?" I demanded to know.

"A few days ago, there was an attack and I lost one of my best soldiers to the dark. It was a horrifying sight to see how he was engulfed in shadow and darkness," she answered willingly.

"I need to know more details about the attack. It's truly of vital importance I know everything."

"Are you heading to the Border Country? This is what the realm is abuzz with?" she commented like a schoolgirl who had just caught the end of an excellent piece of gossip readily available to be spun into gold.

"That's right!" I responded confidently.

"Then I'm guessing your passing through my kingdom was bred from a need for something in particular?" She smartly observed.

Looks like her spy network had grown exponentially since we last saw their kind. She seemed to know an awful lot about my journey which made me think about her motives and doubt her initial willingness to aid me. I remember what my sister had told me some time ago in a private conversation before the feast at the palace only hours ago. She had pointed out that the Siren Queen is most likely to offer me the Dreadful dinner; a sign of their culture that they had converted to the darkness for the battle to come. A weird thing about them was the fact that though powerful, they were easily seduced by the power of darkness and such an offer would most likely be an attempt on my life. I was honestly waiting for her to make the offer. Though the success during this part of my travels was due to my sister I had neglected to congratulate her on her becoming the guardian of the *Beastinomicum*, a book filled with legends and the traits of all sorts of magical creatures. Such a position was only held once a generation by the youngest royal heir. The book was forged at the heart of what would later become the Golden Forest, a sentient being capable of writing itself and adding to its knowledge the more it encountered so that the holder or anyone they desired to would have access to knowledge and be able to anticipate and counter the creatures' actions.

From the moment the queen had started conversing with me I had activated the mental link between my brother and sister so that I would have readily available access to their objective observations especially how everyone's lives depended on me successfully completing my mission. I just had to hold on for three more days and my powers would exponentially grow to new heights on my twenty-fifth birthday, the legal age to assume the throne should a parent was willing to abdicate in Seltra.

Just before the queen was done talking, my brother shared with me through the link that she would, in fact, offer me a dinner she would present as a joyous occasion to celebrate the imminent defeat of the Emperor. He wasn't wrong; she did exactly that to which in a panic mode I accepted.

"Perfect!" she said with an unbecoming joy in her voice.

It was almost like hearing a child react to getting their new toy for which they had been bugging you for months, but your previous objections made you the enemy in their eyes. The queen ordered her servants to prepare the dinner and insisted that she would host me for the night without any mention of what I had come for or my mission. If that wasn't fishy, I don't know what was, but I decided that I wasn't duped nor was I leaving without the best weapon I had against the

Emperor. On the plus side, should there have been the need for battle I knew that my powers were more than a match for her. It's not that she wasn't powerful; it was simply that my powers were heightened and not easily matched by any magic user due to my heritage and station as she would soon find out.

"Your Majesty," I exhaled sharply. "May I retire to one of your bed chambers to prepare accordingly?" I added.

"Of course," she responded. "I will have one of the servants escort you."

"Thank you," I allowed to slip my tongue.

I could see the deception written in her eyes. There is no doubt about her attempting to dispatch me using the feast as an excuse, which she could probably attribute to an attack should there be a need to cover up the execution to my family. Unbeknownst to her, my siblings were right there, and they would rain hell on her should she have succeeded. *She didn't succeed though as you might guess.* Her servant led me into a beautifully decorated room.

"There you go, Majesty," he said.

'Thank you," I responded trying to hold the anger bottled inside.

It wasn't the time nor the place to use it. Immediately after he left the room, I cast a hybrid spell simply by thinking about it; the spell would cloak my movements inside the room only and also give me absolute privacy. The spell I had cast was almost involuntarily, meaning that as I was nearing my ascension day, my magic was growing; every day that passed brought me closer to extreme new powers which I would be able to use against the Emperor, but even that I knew wasn't enough. My sister was almost in awe of how the spell was cast so effortlessly.

"Brother, you're almost ready. Just hold on a little longer. I have a solution… Actually, I have two." She corrected herself on the spot. "I know how you can retrieve the buxus and survive the dinner," she remarked.

"How?" I said. "What do you have in mind?"

"I could shield your body with a spell that will last a few hours in order for it to be able to fight any poison or physical harm. Secondly, I could sense the location of the buxus through you and direct you to its hiding place," she confidently informed me.

"Can you do that?" I doubted.

"You are not the only one with incredible gifts you know," she answered as though I had offended her.

I allowed her to take control of my magic which she utilized by automatically assuming control of my motor skills to cast the spell of protection. My hands came together and gently touched my torso meanwhile a gentle wind hugged my body and tightened around me which dissipated almost instantly.

"It's done," she estimated.

Next, she would access my visual pathways to search for the buxus' magical signature in the vicinity.

What I saw while the spell was being cast, I had not expected. I could peer into the queen's private room; the glow of the buxus was emanating from her chest. *Was she really that vain that she would hide such an artifact inside her?* Her arrogance seemed to know no bounds, but now I knew where it was and also had a rough idea of how I could retrieve it should things go south, which in such instances they usually and unexpectedly do.

"Now, we know where the buxus is and I think I have an idea how to get it when the time is right," my brother interjected.

"What do you have in mind?"

"Promise me you will let me handle it when the time comes," he stated.

"OK. I'm sure you have a pretty good idea how to handle yourself in battle. I trust you," I assured him.

I dropped the spell once I sensed someone from the servants approaching and quickly changed my clothes with a spell. My previous clothes melted into a new and improved appearance appropriate for the occasion. A knocking on the other side of the door meant that acting time was on. The performance of a lifetime would have to be put on to fool her. The servant knocked again and only after I had responded he entered. I exited the room and followed him to what the palace would use as a dining hall for important guests. The queen sat at the head, the rest of the council sat around the table, while I was seated on her right side, as it was customary for her to do whenever she had a royal guest, especially a soon-to-be ruling monarch like me. The servants began bringing the food and serving each one of us separately. Everyone was served almost instantaneously. *At least the service was good despite the intention behind it.*

I have to admit that though I knew how the meal would end, I was determined to enjoy it and play it cool. The meal was succulent, but it was, in fact, laced with a potent poison I could feel in my mouth. Thanks to my sister's spell I felt absolutely nothing other than a slight copper-like aftertaste from every bite. The queen kept chatting me up while I ate and as the time went by she began staring at me in a manner one would only identify as surprised or condemning. She could not believe how the poison didn't even cause me discomfort. I continued as if nothing was happening just to annoy her even more.

After about an hour she had lost all patience and her temperament was starting to change tellingly. I kept pretending as if I knew nothing of her betrayal. Before you can say knife, she stood up and ordered her council to attack me, restrain me and put me in a cell. My brother's turn had come to take over. In an instant I found myself on the other side of the room; my brother had used an acceleration spell that would allow me to move at unperceivable speeds. I readied myself as the council drew their weapons. They marched towards me all at once, but with a swift spell I had immobilized them all completely to the point where they appeared frozen in time. Rings of fire engulfed them, and a barrier was erected around each member that would prevent them from even crossing the boundary if they somehow managed to break free from my spell.

It was the queen's turn to pay for her betrayal. Though I didn't want to set a precedent of killing a ruler in our realm, I had no other choice especially seeing as she wasn't willing to part with the artifact I required, which was also my birthright to wield when the time was right. We danced around each other for hours until her magic betrayed her and allowed me to get the upper hand. Her defeat was exemplary with all her war council watching her slowly decay. Once her magic had run out, I immobilized her and with my right hand covered in flames I reached into her chest, ripped her heart out and retrieved the containment box. With all I needed in hand it was time for me to flee and teleport to the northern kingdom of the Vampire Clans. Just a snap of my fingers and I was there.

I had arrived at the gate of the palace when I noticed an aura above the north keeping the shadow at bay. It was the power I had witnessed from my window before I left Seltra. The vampire elders, who wielding magic as well, had probably combined their power to cast such a powerful containment incantation, and were responsible for buying me the requisite time I needed. The gates opened and two mounted soldiers appeared before me to greet me and escort to the king. *My sister must have tipped them off about my arrival.* Much like with all the vampires in the past, I was met with friendliness and respect. I admired their kind in every possible way. Their intelligence, their ways and strength was something to behold. Of course, they were fierce in battle and not to be underestimated. I hurried to the throne room to meet with the king who had prepared the item I would require before I even asked for it. The king was Laur's father, whom I hadn't seen at first and was quite saddened about. His father and mine were best friends since I can remember, while he had a short fling with my grandmother long before she married my grandfather. During the Great War he had fought by our side; under my grandmother's leadership his armies decimated the enemies with minimal losses for both him and us.

I entered the room and in a flash he appeared before me, and, in typical vampire fashion, he crossed his arms as a way of greeting another royal. His face was the same as I remembered. Not even a single feature had changed.

"Welcome," he exclaimed, filled with joy to see me.

"Thank you for your hospitality," I responded, trying to hold back my tears of glee.

I viewed him as a parent figure in a way.

"You have to tell me everything that happened on your way here," he quipped. "I heard about the Siren queen."

"News travel fast I see," I remarked.

He knew what I had come for. We spent the next minutes catching up as he had sent for the Sword of Creation. The Sword arrived moments later in a case spelt with a protection spell only I could make crumble due to being the rightful heir and future wielder. The sword was the most intricately crafted artifact in the magical realm along with the containment box I had already retrieved. I felt at home in the Clan Palace, many approached me to greet me and converse with me about my family, the upcoming battle and how they were willing to fight by my side when the time came. The vampires' help was at least the one I could most assuredly count on.

The king proposed that I stay at the palace until it was time to move against the Emperor. He would deploy a protection detail if I stepped outside of the palace especially given that I was so close to His lands. It made sense that the closer I moved he would feel my presence more intensely and that his reach would be easier to grip someone close to me. The king came across as truly appreciative and glad to have me in his home. I would spend two days there preparing for the battle ahead. The first night was the most restful I had inasmuch as I was preparing for the battle of my life. The first day we spent strategizing with his lords and generals and I had already asked him to send the message I had composed to the fairies demanding their aid in the final battle which they would not dare disagree with. I based my certitude on how convincing my requests were and that in the past we had stood by them and aided them with countless issues they had faced. Not one of their calls had gone unanswered. *They owed me their allegiance and presence in the battle.*

THE FINAL BATTLE

The next day I awoke from my slumber feeling yet another rush of power indicating that I was but mere hours away from completing my ascension to my rightful place in the magical realm. I dressed myself and headed down to the main hall where much to my surprise I found the Fairy dignitaries who had just been welcomed by Laur and the king. I approached them having fully realized that I had their support and that my message had served its purpose. The king seemed overjoyed at the allies who had just begun to arrive flocking to our location to show their support to me and afford me a fighting chance against the Dark. Just to ensure that I wouldn't stumble upon any surprises, I had spelt the sword and the containment box in place in my room. The spell I had cast was of dual nature. It would protect the objects on one hand and on another I would sense if the spell was tampered with and absorb the magic of the one attempting to break it, making me stronger in the process.

At high noon, the armies of Seltra arrived which was by far the biggest surprise for me. I had asked them to stay away and allow me to complete this task on my own, but this was clearly the work of my brother and sister who had convinced our armies to join the final battle. I rushed to the court to witness the arrival of our armies. The Quattuor mounted four majestic horses, my brother and sister along with my parents rode behind their protectors. The king opened his gates for them, welcomed them into his house and apprised them of the situation and how our defenses would be better coordinated against the Darkness. At night our armies would move against the Border Country where the end of all ends was to be decided. I will keep the battle details to a minimum since I'm guessing all that is of interest to you is the end at this point.

On that day, Laur and I had a heart-to-heart after many years which resulted in us rediscovering our friendship and him pledging to never betray my trust again. I had accepted this turn of events solely on the basis that a vampire was an honorable creature and their promises were not made lightly. He was, in fact, the one who truly saved me in the end albeit not in the way I had chosen. The armies and dignitaries gathered in the massive war room underneath the castle to prepare their armies and strategics, while I decided to head up to the tallest tower of the castle to see where the Elders were casting their protective barrier from. The four of them had joined their magic so neatly, without any holes or cracks. I was amazed by the power they were putting out. Being able to maintain such a spell would be surely destructive for most magic users, but I noticed some strange mental activity from one of them who seemed to be awake from the spell, even though partially. Such a feat should not be possible. I got to thinking and decided that I should investigate further. I entered the mind of the partially awakened Elder. A storm was brewing in his head which made it nearly impossible to focus in there or retrieve him. It didn't take long to discover the reason for the Elder's state. The Dark Emperor had taken control of his mind trying to poison him with his shadow, but he had managed to keep him at bay for days, but the time was now running out. I pushed him out of the Elder's head. He was mad, enraged filled with pure dread that my power had grown exponentially in days.

I pushed him forcefully outside of the Elder's mind. Like a wounded animal he ran. He knew the final battle was real and coming. His end or my end or both would soon be decided by fate. My siblings already knew about this invasion; they met with me minutes later to discuss the Emperor's weakness and how I would best make use of the weapons at my disposal. In the *Beastinomicum*, I witnessed the Emperor's true weakness; the blood of the One was required to end him. In the magical world most things would come in fours, the number of stability, conscientiousness, and determination. In the magical realm as well the realm of Earth, though the number four was one that represented perfection and stability, it was also extremely unlucky, which fitted perfectly in my case. Four elements represented the true weakness of the Emperor, my blood, the Sword of the Creation, the containment box and my life. The last component, though not requisite, it would be claimed, nonetheless. After the discussion with my siblings I admitted the truth to them. Cornelius would have to assume the throne after my death. They weren't really on board, but they had no choice in the matter.

As the armies moved through the night, nature all around us began to wither and die. We reached the Border Country in a few hours. The next hours were critical, but I had a plan. Laur, the Quattuor and I would be the ones going in to face the Emperor while the others would keep the Obsidian nobles and the armies busy. When we reached the Border Country his armies were waiting our arrival like snakes in the grass. The battle didn't take but seconds to ignite after an inspiring speech from the leaders of either side. The battle was bloody and went on for hours. The distracted army of the Emperor was far too busy to notice me, Laur and the Quattuor slipping past them. Those who attempted to stop us met a tragic end at the hands of the Quattuor and Laur who fiercely protected me so that I could conserve my strength for the fight with the Emperor. After an hour of crossing the battlefield, we reach the shadow wall. I took out the Creation Sword, sliced the wall open enough so that we could fit through it. The shadow wall bled out darkness like blood would run from an open wound. Inside the dark dimension I saw shadows and living darkness dancing around every inch. In the distance, the Emperor's throne appeared with him sitting on it. Once he saw me, he launched his attack; covered in obsidian black colors, wielding his broadsword to meet mine as I drew mine as well. We remained locked in battle for Goddess knows how many hours. In a moment of miscalculation, the Quattuor bound him in place while Laur stood guard to prevent any distractions or unwanted visitors. I stepped into the boundary spell, raised my sword and with a single strike I pierced his heart, opened the containment box whose ability to contain magic extended to even godlike creatures and allowed it to suck him into its bottomless dimension.

Leaving the boundary spell, he mastered what remained of his strength to drag me into the containment box with him. The Quattuor and Laur looked on shocked barely having the reflexes or time to react.

Before heading into battle I had given Laur the story of my time from the moment my adventures began to the point they would reach your hands. This book is my gift to you. Don't be sad, dearest Stefania. We all have to walk a path in life and pay the price it demands.

After the end of the final battle Laur visited Earth to leave Stefania the book of my life in Seltra. Such was the end I had met in the dark dimension… or was it?

THE END